Margaret Hillert's

Take a Walk, Johnny

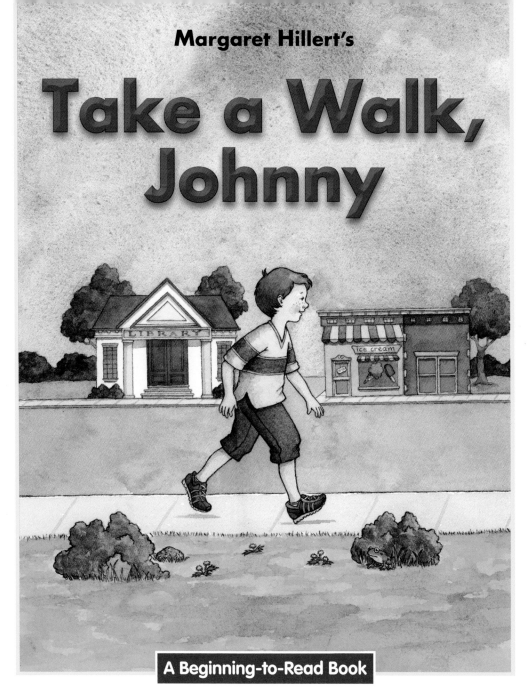

A Beginning-to-Read Book

Illustrated by Rebecca Thornburgh

DEAR CAREGIVER,

The books in this Beginning-to-Read collection may look somewhat familiar in that the original versions could have been a part of your own early reading experiences. These carefully written texts feature common sight words to provide your child multiple exposures to the words appearing most frequently in written text. These new versions have been updated and the engaging illustrations are highly appealing to a contemporary audience of young readers.

Begin by reading the story to your child, followed by letting him or her read familiar words and soon your child will be able to read the story independently. At each step of the way, be sure to praise your reader's efforts to build his or her confidence as an independent reader. Discuss the pictures and encourage your child to make connections between the story and his or her own life. At the end of the story, you will find reading activities and a word list that will help your child practice and strengthen beginning reading skills. These activities, along with the comprehension questions are aligned to current standards, so reading efforts at home will directly support the instructional goals in the classroom.

Above all, the most important part of the reading experience is to have fun and enjoy it!

Shannon Cannon

Shannon Cannon,
Literacy Consultant

Norwood House Press • www.norwoodhousepress.com
Beginning-to-Read™ is a registered trademark of Norwood House Press.
Illustration and cover design copyright ©2017 by Norwood House Press. All Rights Reserved.

Authorized adapted reprint from the U.S. English language edition, entitled Take a Walk, Johnny by Margaret Hillert. Copyright © 2017 Margaret Hillert. Reprinted with permission. All rights reserved. Pearson and Take a Walk, Johnny are trademarks, in the US and/or other countries, of Pearson Education, Inc. or its affiliates. This publication is protected by copyright, and prior permission to re-use in any way in any format is required by both Norwood House Press and Pearson Education. This book is authorized in the United States for use in schools and public libraries.

Designer: Lindaanne Donohoe
Editorial Production: Lisa Walsh

LIBRARY OF CONGRESS CATALOGING-IN-PUBLICATION DATA
 Names: Hillert, Margaret, author. I Thornburgh, Rebecca McKillip, illustrator.
 Title: Take a walk, Johnny / by Margaret Hillert ; illustrated by Rebecca Thornburgh.
 Description: Chicago, IL : Norwood House Press, [2016] I Series: A
  beginning-to-read book I Originally published in 1981 by Follett
  Publishing Company. I Summary: "Johnny is encouraged by his mother to take
  walks to relieve his boredom during the summer. He soon finds joy in
  walking as he collects rocks, goes to the library, finds some coins and
  meets a special friend. Original edition revised with all new illustrations.
  Includes reading activities and a word list"-- Provided by publisher.
 Identifiers: LCCN 2016001839 (print) I LCCN 2016022128 (ebook) I ISBN
  9781599538051 (library edition : alk. paper) I ISBN 9781603579674 (eBook)
 Subjects: I CYAC: Walking--Fiction.
 Classification: LCC PZ7.H558 Tak 2016 (print) I LCC PZ7.H558 (ebook) I DDC
  [E]--dc23
 LC record available at https://lccn.loc.gov/2016001839

288N—072016
Manufactured in the United States of America in North Mankato, Minnesota.

During the school year Johnny got up early every morning. He ate a good breakfast and got dressed. Then he made his bed, cleaned up his room, and went off to school with his friends.

When summer came, school was out. Johnny got up early on the first day of summer. He ate a good breakfast and got dressed. Then he made his bed, cleaned up his room, and looked for something to do.

First Johnny played with his toy cars. Then he made silly faces in the mirror and laughed to see himself.

Next Johnny looked at the plants that were growing in the glass box on the table.

After that he went to his mother and said, "Mother, what can I do now? I don't have anything to do."

Mother said, "Take a walk, Johnny."

So Johnny went out to the yard and
walked around. He saw a bird up
in a tree. He saw a butterfly on a
flower. Then, under the flowers, he
saw a big, brown toad.

"Hello, toad!" said Johnny. "What a
good find you are! You have lots of
bumps and funny eyes. Don't jump
away, toad. I want to take you into
the house and show you to Mother.
She'll be surprised!"

Johnny went into the house. "Mother, look at this toad!" he said. "Isn't he great?"

"Yes," said Mother. "He's a fine-looking toad. Why don't you put him into your glass box with the plants? That would be a good place for him."

The next morning Johnny made his bed, cleaned up his room, and looked for something to do.

First he fed the toad. Then he took the toad out of the box and let him hop around the room.

After that Johnny went to his mother and said, "Mother, what can I do now? I don't have anything to do."

Mother said, "Take a walk, Johnny."

Johnny went out to the yard with his toad. He put the toad back under the flowers.

"Goodbye, toad," said Johnny. "You'll be happier here."

Johnny walked down the sidewalk and looked all around. "I wonder what I'll find today," he said.

Then, under a tree, he saw a rock.

"What a pretty rock," said Johnny. "It has red and white spots, and it even seems to shine a little. I'll take it home and put it with my other rocks."

Johnny went back to his house. "Mother, look at this rock!" he said.

"It's a beautiful rock," said Mother. "I'm glad you found it. You can put it with your other rocks."

The next morning Johnny made
his bed, cleaned up his room, and
looked for something to do.

First he took out all his rocks. Then
he put them all back in boxes again.

After that Johnny went to his mother
and said, "Mother, what can I do
now? I don't have anything to do."

Mother said, "Take a walk, Johnny."

Johnny went outside. "Take a walk.
Take a walk," he said. "That's all
I ever seem to do. But this time I
know where I'll go."

Johnny walked to the library.

"Just look at all the books," he said.
"I can get a book about almost
anything. There are books about
cowboys and wagons, bridges
and mountains, and elephants and
circuses. What a wonderful place
this is!"

Johnny picked out some books and took them home. "Look here, Mother," he said.

"I like to read, and these books are full of good things to read about."

"I see you went to the library," said Mother. "What a good idea! Books are fun to read, and it looks like you found some good ones."

The next morning Johnny made his bed, cleaned up his room, and looked for something to do.

He read for a time. Then he put all his books away.

After that Johnny went to his mother and said, "Mother, what can I do now? I don't have anything to do."

Mother said, "Take a walk, Johnny."

Johnny went outside and began to walk. "Walk, walk, walk," he said. "I'm getting tired of all this walking."

Suddenly he saw something shiny on the sidewalk. "What's this?" he said. "It's money right here on the sidewalk! Now I can run to the ice cream store."

So Johnny ran to the ice cream store.

"Boy, what a great place!" he said. "Just look at all the different kinds of ice cream. There are so many kinds that I don't know which one to pick."

"Take your time," said the man.

"The chocolate looks good," said Johnny at last. "I would like a chocolate ice cream cone."

Johnny ate his ice cream cone
on the way home.

"Mother!" said Johnny. "Guess what I found on my walk this time. I found money! I found money and I got an ice cream cone."

"You did?" said Mother. "The money was a good find, wasn't it?"

The next morning Johnny did all the same things. He ate breakfast. He made his bed. He cleaned up his room.

After that Johnny went to his mother and said, "Mother, I am going for a walk."

His mother said, "Have a good time, Johnny."

Johnny walked and walked and walked. He walked up and down. He walked around and around.

Suddenly Johnny saw a little puppy in the street. "Here, puppy. Here, puppy," he called.

But the puppy did not move out of the street.

Johnny looked both ways for cars. Then he ran to get the puppy out of the street.

"Oh, you poor little thing," said Johnny. "Don't you have a home? You must be lost. I'll bet you need something to eat. Do you want to come home with me? Maybe I can keep you."

Johnny took the puppy home.

"Mother!" said Johnny. "Look what I found on my walk this time. She is so little. I think she is lost. May we keep her, Mother?"

"Well," said Mother. "First let's read the Lost and Found part of the newspaper."

Mother looked in the newspaper.

"No, I don't see anything about a lost puppy in here," she said.

"Now we will make some signs."

Johnny and his mother made signs. The signs looked like this.

They put one sign on a tree. They put another sign in the ice cream store. When they got home, the telephone rang.

"I see you found my puppy," said a man on the telephone. "You can have her. I can't take care of her."

Mother told Johnny what the man had said. "You can keep the puppy, Johnny," said Mother. "She's as cute as a button."

"Cute as a button. Cute as a button," said Johnny. "Oh, Mother. Button would be a nice name for her."

Then Johnny called to the puppy. "Here, Button. Here, Button. Now you are my puppy. We'll be such good friends."

Every morning after that, Johnny
got up early and ate a good
breakfast. Then he made his bed,
cleaned up his room, and went for
a walk with Button.

And sometimes Mother went
walking with them.

Foundational Skills

In addition to reading the numerous high-frequency words in the text, this book also supports the development of foundational skills.

Phonological Awareness: The long /ī/ sound

Sound Substitution: Say the words on the left to your child. Ask your child to repeat the word, changing the short /i/ sound to a long /ī/ sound:

lick=like	hid=hide	bit=bite	mill=mile	lit=light
fit=fight	kit=kite	sit=sight	fin=fine	dim=dime
pick=pike	rip=ripe	Tim=time	knit=knight	

Phonics: The long /ī/ spelling

1. Make four columns on a blank sheet of paper and label each with the spellings for long /ī/: i_e, ie, igh, y

2. Write the following words on separate index cards:

bike	pie	high	sky	shine	tries
tie	my	rice	right	fly	try
cry	cries	side	night	ice	might
fries	fry	rid	bright	time	

3. Ask your child to read each word and place the card under the column heading that represents the long /ī/ spelling in the word.

Fluency: Shared Reading

1. Reread the story with your child at least two more times while your child tracks the print by running a finger under the words as they are read. Ask your child to read the words he or she knows with you.

2. Reread the story, stopping occasionally so your child can supply the next word without looking. For example, *During the school year Johnny got up early every _____* (morning).

3. Have your child reread the story, stopping occasionally for you to supply the next word.

Language

The concepts, illustrations, and text help children develop language both explicitly and implicitly.

Vocabulary: Verb Tenses

1. Write each of the following words on separate index cards:

   walk/walking/walked

   sleep/sleeping/slept

   write/writing/wrote

   hide/hiding/hid

   play/playing/played

   eat/eating/ate

   read/reading/read

   jump/jumping/jumped

   help/helping/helped

   find/finding/found

2. Mix up the index cards and ask your child to group them in verb families. Ask your child to place the verbs in each family according to tense (present, present + ing, past) and read them aloud in order.

3. Put the cards in a paper bag and shake it to mix them up. Take turns selecting cards from the bag and stating sentences using the words.

Reading Literature and Informational Text

To support comprehension, ask your child the following questions. The answers either come directly from the text or require inferences and discussion.

Key Ideas and Detail

- Ask your child to retell the sequence of events in the story.
- What flavor ice cream did Johnny get?

Craft and Structure

- Why did Johnny's mother keep telling him to take a walk?

Integration of Knowledge and Ideas

- Why did Johnny's mother look in the newspaper and help him make signs?
- If you went for a walk in your neighborhood, what are some things you might find?

Take a Walk, Johnny uses the 66 vocabulary words listed below.

This list can be used to practice reading the words that appear in the text. You may wish to write the words on index cards and use them to help your child build automatic word recognition. Regular practice with these words will enhance your child's fluency in reading connected text.

beautiful	early	mirror	school	wagons
bed	elephants	money	shine	wonder
book(s)		morning	shiny	wonderful
breakfast	flower(s)	mountains	sidewalk	
bridges	found		signs	year
bumps	friends	newspaper	something	
butterfly		nice	sometimes	
button	glass		spots	
		other	store	
chocolate	house	outside	street	
circuses			suddenly	
cleaned	ice	plants	summer	
cone	idea	played	surprised	
cowboys		poor		
cream	laughed	puppy	telephone	
cute	library		tired	
	little	rang	toad	
dressed	lost	read		
during		rock(s)		
		room		

ABOUT THE AUTHOR Margaret Hillert has helped millions of children all over the world learn to read independently. She was a first grade teacher for 34 years and during that time started writing books that her students could both gain confidence in reading and enjoy. She wrote well over 100 books for children just learning to read. As a child, she enjoyed writing poetry and continued her poetic writings as an adult for both children and adults.

Photograph by Glenna Washburn

ABOUT THE ILLUSTRATOR Rebecca Thornburgh is a children's book author/illustrator who spends her days drawing whimsical creatures and thinking up stories. She has illustrated over 130 books. When she's not reading or drawing, Rebecca sings with a classical symphonic chorus and a rock band. She lives in a pleasantly spooky Victorian house with her husband and two silly dogs. www.rebeccathornburgh.com.